Flash's Dream

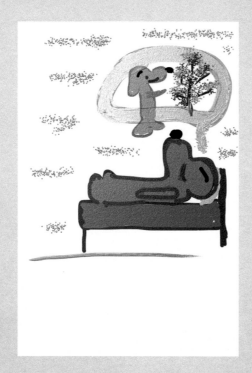

Written by   Charlie Alexander
Artwork by Charlie Alexander

Flash's Dream

Charlie Alexander

Flash fell into a deep sleep.

He saw beautiful scenery all throughout his dream.

He was watching birds fly through the clouds and sky.

Flash smiled and pointed.

One awesome bird landed on a branch right
next to Flash.

It made him smile!

Flash just had to try sitting on a branch too

He laughed out loud when he realized how silly he looked

The flowers smelled so good!

Even if it was just a dream.

The driveway was lined with trees.

They were standing tall and straight!

Flash thought of driving to Washington D.C.

It was an exciting ride!

The Washington Monument was so high!

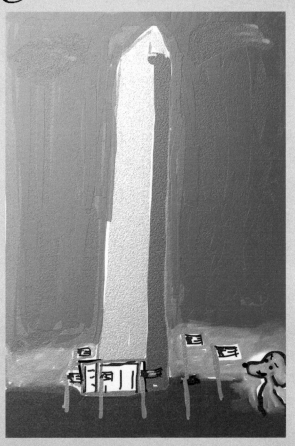

Flash thought it reached the sky.

Flash was truly inspired.

He just had to sing "America the Beautiful"!

It's the White House!

Flash knew this is where our President lives!

It was time to board the train.

Breath taking scenes were waiting for Flash!

The colorful flowers covered the mountainside.

It was spectacular!

Flash couldn't resist standing under the waterfall.

The water was very cold!

Flash just had to try the raft!

After all, he was already soaked!

A nice walk fit right in.

The turtle and fish agreed.

A canoe ride was calming.

Flash loved to paddle.

Surfing a giant wave was exciting!

Keep you're balance Flash.

Flash's eyes were filled with surprise.

He enjoyed the gentle stream!

A hot air balloon ride was a dream!

Flash knew lunch was waiting for him to land.

Turkey and corn were for lunch.

Flash had to go and pick the corn.

The corn was bright yellow!

It smelled so good!

Lying down after lunch was cool.

It was nice to enjoy the flowers and trees.

Of course, Flash dreamed of riding a horse.

It was a dream within a dream!

It was beginning to snow!

Flash could see the snowflakes.

The pond was almost frozen.

The mountains were covered in white and so were the trees.

Of course, Flash had to ski.

He liked his goggles!

It was time to leave.

Luckily Flash had his own airplane.
Even if it was a dream!

Flash loved his dog!

He loved taking him for walks.

It was hammock time!

Flash needed to rest a little.

Flash dreamed of Disney World.

He imagined the castle!

Epcot was so big.

Flash was blown away!!

Flash was coming home.

He could see his house through the trees.

And it was so nice to see Charlie And Becky too!

He knew they'd be waiting.

It was so nice to be back.

After all, there's no place like home!
The End

To order additional copies of this book, contact:
Xlibris
844-714-8691
www.Xlibris.com
Orders@Xlibris.com

ISBN: Softcover   978-1-6698-7546-8
               Hardcover   978-1-6698-7545-1
               EBook   978-1-6698-7544-4

Library of Congress Control Number: 2023907951

Print information available on the last page

Rev. date: 04/25/2023

Printed in the United States
by Baker & Taylor Publisher Services